Kick the Football, CHARLIE BROWN!

By Charles M. Schulz

Adapted by Cordelia Evans

Illustrated by Scott Jeralds

SIMON SPOTLIGHT
New York   London   Toronto   Sydney   New Delhi

SIMON SPOTLIGHT
An imprint of Simon & Schuster Children's Publishing Division
1230 Avenue of the Americas, New York, New York 10020
This Simon Spotlight paperback edition August 2016
© 2016 Peanuts Worldwide LLC
SIMON SPOTLIGHT and colophon are registered trademarks of Simon & Schuster, Inc.
For information about special discounts for bulk purchases, please contact Simon & Schuster Special Sales at
1-866-506-1949 or business@simonandschuster.com.
Manufactured in the United States of America 0917 LAK
10 9 8 7 6 5 4 3 2
ISBN 978-1-4814-6209-9
ISBN 978-1-4814-6210-5 (eBook)

Every year when football season starts, Charlie Brown attempts to achieve one of his many goals in life: to kick a football and watch it soar through the air. And every year when Charlie Brown tries to do this, the same thing happens. It all starts with his friend Lucy.

"Over here, Charlie Brown!" says Lucy. "I've got a brand-new ball. I'll hold it, and you come running up and kick it."

"A brand-new ball!" Charlie Brown shouts. "Wow, this is a real treat."

Charlie Brown gets a running start and approaches Lucy. But just as he goes to kick the ball, Lucy pulls it away. Charlie Brown goes flying into the air and lands with an "AAUGH!" on his back.

"Why did you take the ball away?" Charlie Brown asks Lucy angrily.

"It suddenly occurred to me that if I let you kick it, it wouldn't be new anymore," Lucy explains.

The next time it's the same story.

"Charlie Brownnnnn!" calls Lucy in a singsong voice. "Come on. I'll hold the football, and you come running up and kick it," Lucy says. "I have a surprise for you this year."

A surprise? thinks Charlie Brown. *That must mean she isn't going to pull the football away. She's going to be surprised when she sees how far I kick that ball!*

Just like last year, Charlie Brown runs quickly at the football that Lucy's holding. Just like last year, the second he goes to kick it, Lucy pulls it away. And just like last year, Charlie Brown goes flying into the air and lands with an "AAUGH!"

"And now for the surprise," Lucy says to Charlie Brown, who can't bring himself to get up quite yet. "Would you like to see how that looked on instant replay?"

The next time Charlie Brown sees Lucy holding a football, he won't even give her a chance to talk. "No!" he shouts. "You must think I'm crazy—you say you'll hold the ball, but you won't! You'll pull it away, and I'll fall again."

"Why, Charlie Brown, I wouldn't think of such a thing," insists Lucy, smiling calmly. "I'm a changed person. Isn't this a face you can trust?"

"All right," Charlie Brown agrees begrudgingly. "You hold the ball, and I'll come running up and kick it."

This time Charlie Brown is only a little surprised when Lucy pulls away the football and he lands on his back.

"I admire you," Lucy tells him. "You have such faith in human nature."

So Charlie Brown avoids Lucy. But she knows just where to find him.

"What's up?" Sally asks when she opens the door to her house to see Lucy standing there.

"Tell your brother to come out," says Lucy. "I'll hold the ball, and he can come running up and kick it."

"She's here again," Sally says to Charlie Brown inside. "Why does she think she can fool you over and over?"

"You don't really believe my brother will fall for this, do you?" Sally asks Lucy. "I mean, after all, how often do you think you can fool someone with the same trick?"

But Charlie Brown is already following Lucy outside.

Sally stands on the front stoop and watches as Charlie Brown runs to kick the football, Lucy pulls it away, and Charlie Brown goes flying and lands on his back with an "AAUGH!"

"Pretty often, I guess," Sally remarks as Charlie Brown goes back into the house, his head spinning.

But Charlie Brown is not a quitter—and he is *not* going to give up!
"I'm going to kick that football all the way to the North Pole!" he declares.

His friends are very supportive. They believe in Charlie Brown, too! And besides, they all know how much Lucy loves her tricks . . . and they would love to see Charlie Brown get the better of her.

Linus offers to lend Charlie Brown his blanket as a good-luck charm.

Sally gives Charlie Brown a big, encouraging hug.
"Isn't this part of football, anyway?" she asks, squeezing him tight. "We're practicing right now, big brother!"
"That's tackling, not hugging," says Charlie Brown, gasping for air.

For help training, Charlie Brown turns to
his most trusted friend and adviser: Snoopy.

Snoopy puts him to work, making him run laps to strengthen his legs
and practice drills over and over again. He's a great coach!

After all, Snoopy's had a lot of experience with his own team.

Charlie Brown even has a dream that night that he kicks the football. And not only does he kick it, but it soars higher into the air than any football in the world! Charlie Brown knows he can do this.

The next day Charlie Brown is ready to face Lucy. And she's ready for him. She sets herself up on the grass.

"So, I'll hold the ball, Charlie Brown, and you come running—" she begins.

"Lucy!" Rerun interrupts. "Mom says to come in for lunch."

Lucy ignores her little brother and turns back to Charlie Brown. "You come running up and kick it—"
"She says right now!" shouts Rerun.
"Oh, good grief!" says Lucy.

"That's all right. We'll do it some other time," says Charlie Brown. He's getting a little nervous anyway.

"No, Rerun can take my place," says Lucy, handing him the football. She goes inside.

"Me?" says Rerun. He kneels on the grass and holds the football steady.

This time I'll do it! thinks Charlie Brown. *Rerun would never pull the ball away!*

"Here we go!" he shouts, gearing up to run at the ball.

A few minutes later Rerun carries the football inside to where Lucy is eating her lunch.

"What happened?" she asks. "Did you pull the ball away? Did he kick it?"

Rerun smiles mysteriously. "You'll never know."